T0210090

# Labyrinth of Love

VERONIKA

authorHOUSE

*AuthorHouse™*
*1663 Liberty Drive*
*Bloomington, IN 47403*
*www.authorhouse.com*
*Phone: 1 (800) 839-8640*

*© 2019 Veronika. All rights reserved.*

*No part of this book may be reproduced, stored in a retrieval system, or transmitted*
*by any means without the written permission of the author.*

*This is a work of fiction. All of the characters, names, incidents, organizations, and dialogue in*
*this novel are either the products of the author's imagination or are used fictitiously.*

*Published by AuthorHouse 06/29/2019*

*ISBN: 978-1-7283-1793-9 (sc)*
*ISBN: 978-1-7283-1792-2 (e)*

*Print information available on the last page.*

*Any people depicted in stock imagery provided by Getty Images are models,*
*and such images are being used for illustrative purposes only.*
*Certain stock imagery © Getty Images.*

*This book is printed on acid-free paper.*

*Because of the dynamic nature of the Internet, any web addresses or links contained in this book may have changed*
*since publication and may no longer be valid. The views expressed in this work are solely those of the author and do*
*not necessarily reflect the views of the publisher, and the publisher hereby disclaims any responsibility for them.*

This is sunny Los Angeles where dreams comes true, sleepy Jennifer slowly wakes up in her bedroom,yawning, she crawls out of bed to start the day.

She goes down up stairs to the kitchen, she dressed in comfy pajamas, she heads downstairs, still barely awake. Her cute dog spitz Mickey meets her at the bottom of the stairs and she pats him lovingly on the head.

Hey Buddy -Jenny meets her dog and then heads to the kitchen with the dog in tow.

Entering the kitchen, she sees her mom affront of the kitchen and cooking something.

- Hey dear, would you like something to eat? – asks Jenny`s mom

- No thanks mom - tells Jenny looking at her mom. Jenny sits at the kitchen table. After a small beat Jenny asks her mom

- By the way what`s time the lawyer?

- At 5 pm honey.

- Ok I`m gonna take a shower.

Jenny comes from the table, and goes back to the stairs. Her mom looks at her and answers her loudly

- Ok,hurry up!

On the same day Jenny and her mom and her mom walk along the notary's corridor. Jennifer looks at her mum

- I'm so excited about what grandmother bequeathed to me, her mom Lucie smiles

- We will know very soon honey...be patient, beat. Jenny's mom opens the main door of the notary's department and they go to the front desk.

- Good evening, we have a time with a lawyer, reception worker smiles

- Hello, could i have your name please?

- Yes sure,Lucie Walter and my daughter Jennifer Walter

Notary receptionist typing on computer,and then looks at Jenny and her mum

- Ok... sit down please, lawyer is going to come as soon as its possible. Jenny looks at her

- Ok Thank you, Lucie looks at Jenny

- Lets go Jenny,lets sit

Jenny and her mom go out from reception desk and at that time lawyer comes

Hello Walter`s family, nice to meet you, thank you for coming-tells lawyer . Jenny`s mom shook hands with a lawyer.

- Good Afternoon mister Smith, nice to meet you too! This is my daughter Jennifer- she introduces Jenny to the lawyer and he looks at Jenny and shook her hand with a smile

Nice to meet you young lady, well lets go to my office please -smiles mister Smith.

They are all together in the notary office sitting at one round table. Lawyer gives to Jenny all documents and she looks at them. Jenny`s mom looks at Jenny

Well,well...what`s there? Beat. Jenny opens the envelope and reads with a surprises

What? I`m gonna be the owner of my grandmother`s magazine « 5 fashion ideas!» Wait... this company is in New York...Its in New York! But I`m in Los Angeles... oh my God... her mom surprises

- O my God! Jenny! Are you happy?

- Well, I don`t know what to say,I mean... NEW YORK! New city for me, so I don`t know what to say. Mom, it means that I have to move there right? Oh...

- Well, Yes...but I believe in you! You are the great writer! And your uncle lives there so he could help you there! -tells with consider Lucie

Jenny sits in shock looking at her mom.

- Ok, I know that it is not an easy decision... you could think about it at home...and come back-tells Mr Smith

Jenny stands up from the table she confuses.

- Yes, you right... Lets go mom...and, thank you for all information Mr Smith – tells Jenny and looks at the lawyer.

- Yes thank you! -tells Lucie to lawyer.

- You very welcome Mrs and miss Walter!-tells with a smile lawyer.

On the next free day Jenny sits on the terrace on the couch with a computer and searches the information about her grandmother`s magazine. Jenny`s mother looks at her from the living room with smile and comes to her.

- What are you doing dear?-asks wondering, Jenny`s mom.

- Oh, I`m...I get acquainted with my grandmother's publishing house-answers Jenny to mom.

- Wow, so you`ve made a decision? Jenny looks at her mom.

- YES-tells with consider in her eyes Jennifer.

Jenny`s mom smiles and hugs Jenny.

- Its gonna be your new life...tells Jenny`s mom.

- I hope so-tells Jenny

Exiting Jennifer comes to the airport sits in the airplane, and to her comes stewardess

- Good morning! How are you today? Would you like something to drink? -asks stewardess to Jenny

  Yea! Give me whisky please, I fly to the another city alone, and ALSO I finds out that I`m new owner of big company! Thanks God, I know a lot about this fashion industry-tells Jenny

- Oh this is awesome ! What type of business?

- Fashion… magazine-tells Jenny to stewardess

- Ooo... its interesting

- Yea...

At this time, another steward asks another passenger to fasten a seat belt, but he doesn`t listen.

- Ser,could you please fasten your sit belt

- Yes,sure... -tells with the smile passenger

Steward moves to the other side of the plane, but that passenger doesn`t faster his belt. Steward comes back to him, and notices that he still doesn`t fasten sit belt and that passenger doesn`t hear him again is in headphones.

Steward becomes angry and calls the police. Police come to the airplane and come to this passenger. Passenger pays attention and takes off his headphones.

- Sorry what happens?

- Could you please leave the airplane -tells police.

- Why? I`m not even drunk!

- You don`t follow my rules- tells steward to passenger.

Passenger leaves the airplane. Jennifer notices that police inside the airplane and wondering asks steward

- Sorry,what happened? why have you called the police? Steward looks at Jenny

- Because one of the passenger doesn`t follow the rules! I told him twice to fasten sit belt! He even doesn`t listen. Jennifer surprising looks at steward.

- Strange

- You want to be next? Jenny smiles

- Oh no!

Steward walks away from Jenny. By the way Jennifer stops another steward.

- Oh,Im sorry,double whiskey to me please.

A few days later... Its another busy, noisy day in New York. Confident Jenny drives at job in her white mercedes car. She is a hardworking, honest and friendly young women of twenty -five years old. She parks her car, climbing the stairs on her heels with smile.

Jenny enters the lobby of the building of her company greets the security

- Good Morning Miss Walter-tells with a smile security worker

- Good Morning Mark, how are you?

- Good thanks,you are in rush? As always?

- Oh, Yes, rush is my second name... I guess... -tells Jenny with a smile.

By the time she waits for an elevator. She nervously presses the elevator button several times.

- Come on... Oh... Ok see you Mark!

Elevator opens.

Jennifer reaches the floor of her company and she enters to the company on the top of the New York`s building. She walks with confidence in herself, she goes through the reception desk where

her worker tells her that her new employee John is already waits her in her office for his interview, he is already there.

- Jennifer, Mrs John Perunni already waits you in your office-tells to Jennifer,Mellissa.

- Thanks Melissa, I`m coming.

- Ok,I will tell him

Jenny walks into her office without showing that she is late to sit in her chair greeting John with a smile.

- Good Morning John! Well, sorry to be late, you know its NYC traffic, not that I late every time...only sometimes...

John looks at her.

- Well,no matter,anyway! Lets talk about yourself John, what brings you to our fashion company?

- Oh its ok, my pleasure to be here, don`t apologize Miss Jenny Walter-tells John with a smile.

- Well,I have experience of working in a magazine. I`m from Italy, I am Italian.

Its good that you have there an experience.

- Thank you Miss Jennifer! I`ve always dreamed of moving to New York and when I saw the vacancy on the assistant to the chief editor of the fashion magazine, I thought that this is destiny! Well, more to precisely say, this is my chance. Hah ...

Jenny scrolls through John`s portfolio.

- Alright...I see, you have been working for a 5 years in a playboy magazine... it has been the very first thing that impressed me...in your resume...John. John smiles

- I really glad to hear it dear Jennifer.

- Ok,are you ready to work full time?

- Yes of course,its not too much for me, I used to it- joyfully answers John.

- Ok, and now the main question: what do you think about perfume?- asks Jennifer to John

Beat

- Do you personally use them? We usually write about them! I personally wear men's perfume sometimes- tells Jennifer with a smile by showing to John perfume box.

- Well, since I'm Italian, I wear them too, man's... which is not surprising-tells John

- Sound cool! So...let go! I will show you our company !

John and Jenny walk through the corridors of the company. Jenny goes to the dining room where the staff is having lunch at that time and introduces John.

- Good Afternoon everyone! Let me introduce you my intern John! He is from Italy, please love and respect him.

- Oh really? Hi everyone! Nice to meet you guys! Oh it happened! Thank you dear Jenny. I will not let you down-joyfully tells John to Jennifer.

Jenny guides John down the elevator.

- I hope you will enjoy working in our company, because I really need a lot of help and glad to tell you, you are officially worker of our company " five fashion ideas".

- Yes I will Jennifer.

Beat.

- Well, see you tomorrow at 10am. I will send you all information and time by email.

John smiles and left into elevator.

On the hardworking morning of Monday Jenny goes to the coffee machine by the song Bee Gees - Stayin 'Alive. Where is John also there preparing for himself coffee. Jenny comes closer to John and sniffs his collar.

- Boss...

John frozes in surprise. His eyes were filled with happiness. He has a smile on his face. It seems to him that Jenny is flirting with him.

- Hugo Boss... I can notice that you wear it right now.

- Oh, you're talking about perfume...boss...hah and you really know about perfume, now this perfume is on me- confusedly answers John.

- You know I usually wear them.

Jenny suddenly looks at her watch.

- Ok John I have to go, I just came here to tell you don't forget to do new release statistics please. Ok See you.

And so Jenny quickly runs away from the dining room.

Ok! And for you too a good day! My lovely Boss- Loudly answers John to Jenny.

Jenny goes back to her office where there waits her aunt Michelle with representative of perfume line

Jenny enters her office with a surprise on her face.

- Hello Michelle, nice to see you, thanks for coming

- Hey Jenny, thanks for coming on time- joyfully tells Michelle to Jennifer

Michelle introduces Jennifer to the representative

- Sofia, this is my niece Jennifer and also the editorial owner of «5 fashion ideas» magazine.

Jennifer greats representative.

Good Afternoon, nice to meet you- smiles Jennifer

- Good Afternoon Jennifer, nice to meet you too, we want to show you our shop because we workswith your grandmother's magazine already 5 years-tells with a smile Sofia.

- Yes I would love to work with you too!

- So we have to go there right now -interrups Michelle

- Right now right? Ok- tells Jennifer

On the same day Jenny walks with Sofia though the perfume shop and Sofia shows her with which perfumes the magazine already have worked.

- As you see Miss Jeniffer we have a lot of different odors-tells Sofia by showing one of the perfume to Jennifer.

- Jenny takes from shelf one of their perfume names- «day of Beauty» and smells it.

- Hm, yes its smells so good

- Could you choose something from our new collection for your new issue of magazine?-tells Sofia

Jenny shows to Sofia that perfume that she holds and just smells

- Yes sure, this perfume from new collection?-asks Jennifer

- Oh no, sorry, but next to it is new collection. By the way, let me show you-tells Sofia

Sofia takes from the same shelf another perfume and gives it to Jenny

- Try this!

Jenny takes this perfume and smells.

- I think, there are notes of lavender, cinnamon and strawberry essence-tells Jenny

- Wow you guess it 100 percent!

Well I'm perfume addicted, so of course I will guess, but thanks that you notice that I'm right- proudly tells Jennifer.

- You very welcome dear Jennifer! Its really pleasure to start working with you Jennifer.

- My pleasure too.

Suddenly comes Michelle to this shop.

- Wow Jenny! You impressed me! No wonder that chose you as the heir to the magazine- tells Michelle

Jenny smiles.

- Ok, let's sign up new contract between you and us Miss Jennifer.

- Sure! – tells with a smile Jenny.

Jennifer, Michelle and Sofia sits at one round big table, and Michelle gives to Jenny documents that Jenny should sign up,Jenny reads it

- This is agreement for our long-term cooperation-shows Sofia.

Jenny signs it up.

- Ok, oh and there to sign too?

- Yes, here as wel-tells Sofia to Jennifer.

Jennifer gives back one copy of agreement to Michelle and one keeps for herself in her folder.

- Great! A new smell of success ladies.

- Yes- joyfully tells Sofia.

Jenny smiles.

Jenny walks though the corridor to the photo studio.

Photographer Christina takes a pictures of one of the model for the Jenny's magazine

- Hey Christina how its going?

Christina turns to Jenny with a with camera.

- Oh hey dear how are you? Yes we are working-smiles Christina to Jennifer.

- I'm good thank you, glad to see that work goes on.

- I gonna go for a coffee right after photoshoot want to join me?- tells Christina.

- Yes why not! I have time right now...

- By the way I have a great idea to make photoshoot with you, you don't mind?- joyfully tells Christina to Jennifer during her work.

- You mean me instead of model?- laughs Jenny.

- Right! Only on one page.

- Sounds great, I would love to!

- Good- smiles Christina.

Its evening at Jenny`s apartment,Jennifer looks at her phone, and thinks to pick up her phone and call to John.

IJohn`s old friend Tom from school lives sometimes in his apartment, so while John in bathroom Tom sees John`s phone ringing and he answers.

- Hello!?- answers Tom

- Hey...John?- surprising answers Jenny

- Oh no, its Tommy! John is in bathroom right now – answers Tom laughly.

- Oh,okey...could you tell him that his boss calls him and that he could call me back?

- Yeah! Sure.

- Great, thank you! -answers Jenny drinking glass of wine with surprises eyes

Tom hangs up and John comes out from the bathroom with good mood and looking at his friend Tom.

- Hey! By the way, your boss called.

- Oh really? interesting...and? you picked up?- surprisely answers John.

- Yes...she told you to call her back

- Ok- answers John to Tom.

One of the Jenny's photographer in company Christina, young lady with ginger hair comes from office to call to her sister. She looks around so that no one overhears her.

- Hey Liz, how are you dear? Yes...Of course! I will take this folder from her office. For sure, your magazine is way better than her...No, nowhere is video, I checked, this stupid J hasn't put any cameras so I'm sure she hasn't have any in her office too. Ok see you, bye – quietly speaks on phone Christina.

Christina smiles and goes back to office building.

On the next day Jenny walks to the coffee bar and decides to look at herself in one of the car's door window, haven't known that there is sitting John.

- Oh Miss Walter what a surprise to see you here-smiles John

Jennifer is shy because of unexpected situation.

- Yes for me too...I haven't known that I will see you here too, I always come here to this coffee bar

- Could I join you ?

- Yes sure- answers Jenny to John

John goes on his way to work and sees another magazine with Jenny's ideas about a new perfume smell in a kiosk. And in shock runs to tell about it to Jenny buying one of them.

By the way Jennifer sits at her office in front of her computer and John enters.

Knock-knock

- Miss Walter! Miss Walter! Oh... look I haven't know about it, please... look at this!

John gives to her magazine, Jenny stands up.

- Oh my God! What the hell! How it could happened!

- I really don't know!-hysterically answers to Jenny John.

Jenny quickly opens camera program on her computer scrolling surveillance camera back on other days. And there she sees how Christina enters into her office and took the folder.

Jenny runs to looking for Christina, Jenny find her in dining room where are another workers too.

- Christina!!!What the hell are you doing! You secretly collaborate with another magazine?

- Sorry?- smiles Christina

- You know what I mean... cheater.

- You know what, I did it already, my sister's magazine much better than yours! And you can`t do anything with it.

- Your sister's magazine is cheater! ITS BULLSHIT! Oh, and you won`t stolen our ideas anymore, you are fired!

- I don't care!- loudly tells Christina to Jennifer.

- Well, let's see whose magazine will be better!Because you are only photographer and you can`t fully help to your sister anymore-smiles Jennifer.

Workers tells shouted off the liar and Christina left the door slammed. Jenny comes to John`s office and hugs him, John is very happy that Jenny hugs him.

- Oh John, thank you very much that you helped me, I should to watch video surveillance more often in my office.

- Welcome Miss Walter, I told you that I won't let you down.

Jenny smiles to John.

A few days later

Jenny wakes up and her mom knock the door, Jenny opens the door and there is her mom with balloons.

- Surprise! Happy Birthday to my Birthday Girl!-tells Jenny`s mom to Jenny.

- Oh mom,you are here! in New York!Thank you for coming.

Jenny's mom enters into Jenny's house and Jenny opens wine and then goes to her room to bring two dresses for her party.

- Red or White?-asks Jenny.

- Oh... red one!

- Oh mom, I'm already 25 and I still don't have relationship- sighs Jennifer.

- Honey, I understand, but you are so selfsufficient, you still have everything ahead.

- Yes, but I need a person, who will love me and support me...but I really confuses who it could be, man or women- tells Jennifer.

- Oh dear, I know...but listen to me honey, you will see it...I'm sure!

- I hope so-smiles Jenny to her mum and hugs her.

On the evening of the same day Jenny sits in her chair with her computer in her and hears how her mum speaks with her friend Sofia

- Yes Sofia, its great idea! Ok but, I need to ask about it to Jenny! Yes… we gonna celebrate her Birthday in Miami...ok, call you later.

*Veronika*

Beat. Jenny comes to her mum in living room.

- What to ask?- wondering asks Jennifer.

Jenny and her mum sit in the table with a cup of tea.

- Jenny, you remember Mark?

- Yes, we have been playing in childhood together...

Jenny rolls her eyes and sighs.

- What? He is a great guy, by the way he became so handsome right now.

- Might be, and? -sighs Jenny.

- And he lives in Miami, he will be on your Birthday. You dont mind?

- You sure to invite him?

- Yes, he is family friend-tells with a smile Lucie.

- Oh ok...

On the morning Jenny's phone rings, Jenny picks her phone with unfamiliar number

Hello?- surprising

- Hey! Its Mark!

- Oh hey Mark, Sofia`s son?

- Yes! Do you remember me?

- Yes...how to forgot my chidhood- rolls eyes Jennifer.

- Yes, how are you?- flirty tells Mark to Jenny

- I'm great thank you and what about you?

- Im Great as always! You know its nice to hear you again since so long period.

- Me too- quietly asnwers Jenny.

- So, we are friends again?

- Yes, why not

Beat.

- Oh, Mark, I have to go, talk to you later, have a nice day!

Mark looks at Jenny's picture with him in childhood while he speaks with her.

- Ok Jenny-Benny, you remember I called you that?

- Yes...of course I remember such things, ok bye.

- Ok see you.

- Mom!-Louldy tells Jenny.

Jenny comes to her room where is her mom.

- Can I ask one question?

- Yes sure honey.

- Who gave my number to that Mark?

Lucie brushes her hair and looks at Jennifer.

- Me?

- Oh I knew it!

Beat

- And Why did you do that? You know I can't stand him?

Lucie put her brush away and touches Jenny's shoulders.

- Look, you know me and his mom, we are friends, and this family really respect you.

- But-tells Jennifer and Lucie interrupts her.

- And his mom asks your number because her son wants to become friends with you like in childhood, you were good friends! Don't you?

- Yes, but it doesn't mean that we could be friends for real, cause we even don't have topics to discuss, you know.

- I know but listen.

Jenny and her mum sits down on Jenny's bed.

- You and him are adult enough people, he is a writer too... by the way might be it could be interesting just to discuss your simmilar job, you know-tells to Jennifer Lucie.

- Well, who knows, but, only job!- exclaims Jennifer.

- Yes why not, but you know he becomes so handsome man, who knows might be you will like him honey, you told me that you want someone to support you and you want to love somebody, and you confuse, so I'm your mother and I want to help you!- tells with a smile Lucie.

- Yes, thank you mom, but it wont happened, I know myself and I know that, that kind of men as a Mark wont ever be my valentine.

- Jenny...

- I'm sure -Jenny interrupts her mom.

Birds are singing, peaceful area, Jenny comes out from her house and lights a cigar where at the same moment a young slim girl parks on a white Toyota jeep opposite her house by music Bob Marley - Could You Be Loved. Jenny looks at her with big love eyes. This lady comes out from her car in the sunny day in slow motion. Swinging her luxurious blond hair. And closes her car walks into her new house.

- Hey! Neighbor!-exclaims Jenny, but her neighbour doesn`t hear her.

- Hey Blondie!-Jenny repeats.

That lady turns and looks at Jenny, Jenny comes closer to her.

- How could I help you?-asks with a smile that lady.

- Hello! I notice that I haven't seen you before, so nice to meet you, I'm your neighbor. What's your name?-joyfully tells Jenny.

- Oh, nice to meet you too! I'm Sammie, I have bought this house week ago.

They smiles to each other.

- That's good- whispers Jenny.

- Sorry?-asks Sammie.

- I said...Sounds good!

- Oh Ok!-laughs Sammie.

- Well, if you need help... you could always call me! if you want...

Sammie smiles to Jenny

- Yes, sure why not!

- Ok,my number is… -Jennifer spells her shows her number in her phone.

Sammie writes down Jenny's number on her phone.

- Seven,three.... Ok! Nice to meet you once again.

Jenny smiles to Sammie.

- See you then!-tells Jenny and crosses the street to her house and turns to Sammie to wave her. After Jenny enters her home and closes the door.

Jenny walks to coffee bar to her job and suddenly she decides to look at car's door window thinking that no one is in this car but suddenly Johns slowly opens the window in his car Jenny surprises when she realizes that its John's car.

- Good morning Miss Walter, glad to see you affront of my car.

- Oh, I haven't seen you, is this your car?-surprises asks Jennifer.

- Yes its my car, I'm not too, not to have a car-smiles John.

- I know, just asking.

John interrupts Jenny's speech.

- So you came here to have coffee? with me?

- Well, yes, but I haven't known that you will be here... but why not, lets go!

John comes from his car and they goes to the way to coffee bar.

Jenny comes to Sammie with the bottle of wine and knock to Sammie`s door. Sammie opens the door.

- Surprise!

- Jenny!

- Hey, I thought we could celebrate yours housewarming...together!

Well, sure, come in- says Samantha bewildered.

Jenny looks at Sammy's perfume shelf.

- Lancome... I like it... you have a good taste of perfumes...

- I know... those my favorite one... my girlfriend gave me them...1 year ago...

Jenny abruptly turned to Sammy with surprise

- I knew it-whispers Jenny.

- Ha? You always speaks too quietly that I can hardly hear you-tells Sammie gives to Jenny glass of wine.

- Oh sorry, I say I surprises that you are lesbian! I`m I right? You told about your girlfriend?

- Yes...We broke up 6 months ago, oh...I have never loved someone so much as her...I really miss her. -But... what happened?

- We often argued that she was always dissatisfied with something... Jenny and Sammie sit on the sofa together and continue to drink rose wine.

- Oh dear, I'm so sorry about it... Beat.

- Oh my God, I can't believe in it!

- In what?- smiles Samantha.

- That you are lesbian!- joyfully says Jenny.

Sammie surprises and takes Jenny's hand.

- Yes, what about you?

- Well, I'm bisexual...but I also had a girlfriend.

- Nice- says Samantha.

- You know, I am very happy that you understand me! I'm happy that I could finally tell somebody about this.- says Jenny.

Sammie smiles to Jenny.

- Yes, you could always tell me whatever you want!-says Samantha to Jenny.

- Thanks for coming dear, hope to see you again.

- Oh, me too!- says Jennifer.

They hugs each other and Jennifer goes home.

On the next day Jenny stands in her underwear brushing her teeth in her bathroom and suddenly she receives a text message on the phone from Sammie- Jenny...would you like some morning coffee with me on Sunday? Jenny replies with a smile- Yes, when? Sammie-right now. Jenny smiling at her message runs to dress.

Jenny comes to Sammie`s house, Sammie opens the door.

- Hey!

Sammie randomly kisses her, Jenny surprises.

- Wow, Sammie, you are so good kisser, I like it.

- I haven't known that you...like me-tells Jennifer to Sammie.

Yes, I do...but I know that you are bisexual and I'm lesbian, so who knows you might become in love with man secretly of me-laughly says Sammie.

- Sammie,I like you too! I like how you kiss me, but yes, you are right, who knows...

- Yes-smiles Sammie.

- You know, I have new friend and he is so handsome, I wish I could be with him, but I think he is gay.

- Why?

- Because when I called him, his phone took a guy, late at night.

- Ooo, its seriously.

- Yes,that's why I confuses.

Sammie stands up from bed and tells her

- I'm gonna do for us some coffee.

- Okey...

Jenny looks around Sammie's bedroom and sees on the shelf a box of books and albums. Jenny decides to take a school album from the shelf and opens it and sees that Sammie studied in LA in one school with her! Jenny randomly sees herself on one of the school's photo with Sammie in childhood. Jenny puts her hand to her mouth and tears flows from her eyes... she cannot believe her eyes! They were classmates! At that time Sammie comes with two cups of coffee to her bedroom.

- I thought you would like coffee without milk, so I made without. But if you want I could add milk too. Beat.

What happens honey... why you are crying-surprises Sammie.

Jenny looks at her.

- Sammie...you was my classmate, and I haven't seen you for a seventeen years and you also from Los Angeles like me! And your last name is Lopez right?

- O my God, YES! Oh its can't be true, I can't believe...

- Dear! Its true!-says Jenny and stands up from Sammie`s bed and comes closer to Sammie.

- I cant believe too... you have changed beyond recognition...another color of hair, I guess plastic surgery too...but it make sense why we didn't recognize each other. We only saw each other in childhood.

- And,then I moved to New York with my family-says Sammie with tears.

They hugs each other with tears on their eyes.

- We met each other in childhood and now...now you are my neighbour... unbelievable...

- Do you remember Susie mocked me and you stood up for me-says Samantha.

- Yes! Oh my God-laughs Jenny.

- I'm so happy to meet you again dear.

- John won't believe me-whispers Jenny.

- Who?

- My friend from work, whom I like...I guess...

- Oh,ok. Beat.

- Un-be-li-evble- smiles Jenny.

- Yes!

Jenny already at home and suddenly John calls to Jenny, she pickes up phone with a smile.

- Hey dear

- Hey! Where are you?

- I am at home, what about you?

- Could we meet?- says John with serious intonation.

Someone knocks to Jenny's house.

- Oh yes, but... when?

- Right now, why not?

Jenny opens the door and there is Sammie again, Jenny puts phone call on loudspeaker. Jenny surprises why Sammie comes to Jenny when they have met each other today already. Beat.

- Hey do you hear me?-asks John on phone

- Yes John! One second!

- Ok

John is listening how Jenny speak with Sammie

- Hey dear, Jenny, you forgot your scarf after our stormy morning.

- Oh yes, thank you dear-laughly says Jenny.

John surprises after what he hears and at that moment his friend enters his room.

- Jenny, its ok we could meet next time.

- Are you sure?

- Yes

- Ok have a good evening!-joyfully says Jenny.

- I'm sure, bye-sadly says John

John hangs up the phone. Beat.

- John, where is your DVD with box?- asks Tom

- I don't know, actually.

- What happens?

- I talked to my boss, Jennifer, and I want to invite her on a dinner, but I think she has a girlfriend-sadly says John.

- Oh man, do you like her?- Tom says with surprise.

- Yes, a lot-says with a smile Tom.

- So you think she is lesbian?

Yes it might be true-sighs John

- Do you want to go out to drink something?

- Yes,lets go Tom.

John stands up from his bed. Tom comes closer

- Don't give up, might be she is not even lesbian, you never know-says Tom.

On another day Tom drives randomly in one bus with Sammie and she speaks on phone about John and Jenny.

- Yes, she thinks that he is gay, but she likes him...John is her new worker, What? Oh lets see... yes...ok call you later I need to get out, its now my stop.

Tom gets out too, and follows Sammie.

- Lady! Wait please!-exclaims Tom

- Oh, what do you want?

- I'm sorry, but you have spoken about John, it might be my friend!

- Oh really? And what?

- No you don't understand! We need to talk,could we have a cup of tea?-says Tom to Sammie.

Tom and Sammie in the coffee bar sit together.

- So you want to say that he likes Jenny and he is not a gay at all? And and you are his old friend who just live with him for a while?-says with surprise Sammie.

- Yes!

- So you are not his boyfriend?-laughly says Sammie.

- Not at all...I prefer women-says with a smile Tom.

- Me too! Beat.

Tom looks at Sammie with surprise, at this moment the waiter offers them free Champagne.

- It's free?-asks Sammie.

- Yes,because of our opening.

- Wow-smiles Tom.

Tom and Sammie take a glass of champagne and clink glasses.

- Chears!

- Chears-smiles Sammie to Tom.

After a few minutes... Tom and Sammie are drunk.

- It was a bad idea to drink two glasses more, Sam...

- Oh who cares Tom!

- As I understood,that Jenny likes John too?

- Yes, but I like her too, but she is bisexual and she chose to like John, not me... unfortunately...

Beat.

- Sammie! I have an idea! John likes Jenny and she likes him, but they both think that they are homosexual...I suggest to let them know that they like each other!

- No don't tell it right now...lets see when its gonna be a good moment to tell them.

Tom smiles to Sammie.

- I'm in!

Jenny sits affront of her computer, and tries to concentrate of her work but she tired and pulls up,and decides to go to her facebook page and suddenly she sees there friend request, she goes to that account and realizes that this account is of her dad, she surprising accept him to be friends there and goes to the kitchen to pour a glass of wine for herself and sits back to the chair with computer,she smiles and then her dad types.

- O My God!- exclaims Jennifer.

Suddenly her mom overhears her and shouts back to her from another room.

- What happens there?

Jenny shouts her back.

- Nothing!

By the way Jenny`s dad writes her- Dear Jenny, i have lost contact with your mother because we divorced,so she did not allow me to see you, and now I suddenly have found you this is so important for me, I hope you will answer to me how are you,are you happy? everything is ok? With Love,your dad George.

Jenny replies to him - Dear Dad, I'm so happy to know that you've found me, I'm good! I still cant believe that I'm texting you, With Love,Jenny

Jenny makes her food and hears her phone ring. She takes her phone and sees unfamiliar number there.

- Hello?

- Hey Jenny-flirty says Mark.

- Oh Mark,hi ones again.

- How are you?

- I'm good,what about you,Mark?

- I'm good too, listen, I just called to ask do you have boyfriend?

Jenny rolls her eyes and takes ice cream from her kitchen table

- No

- Nice- flirty says Mark.

- No its not nice! I will have, and I will invite you on my wedding.

- Oh might be I will be your fiancé- joyfully.

- Mark please don't tell it! You are my friend!

- Ok, talk to you later then.

- I don't think so

Jenny sighs and put her ice cream back to her kitchen table and went to her mom

- Mom! This Mark calls me again!- exclaims Jenny.

Jenny's mom loudly answers her from another room

- Its great!

- No its not!

i won't answer to his calls anymore!

Beat

- What can I do Jenny?

- Nothing! I'm just angry

- It will pass!- smiles Lucie

- No!

- Well, will see... who knows, its life, young lady.

Jenny goes out from the kitchen room.

A few days later,Jenny stands affront of the mirror on her Birthday in Miami, in her hotel room, she looks at herself in her new long red dress when suddenly she hears ring of her phone in her bag, she takes her phone and smiles that John calls to her.

- John? Hey!-joyfully answers Jennifer.

John stays in his office joyfully speaks with Jenny.

- Hey! Happy Birthday my dear boss!

- Thank you my best intern-smiles Jenny.

John nervously touches the cube rubik from the desk during the speach on the phone.

- How is Miami?

Jenny nervously plays with her dress while she speaks on phone.

- Its good and how is my company there? On the other part of USA-says with a smile Jenny.

- Oh its great. Beat. Jenny,I want to ask you something,if you don't mind.

- Yes,sure,ask!

- Are you lesbian?

Jenny sits on her hotel bed.

- No,I mean almost,I'm bisexual,I had a girlfriend but now I know,that I like only men... but why do you ask about it?

- Oh once I called you and I overhear your conversetion with your friend,I guess... and she told you one funny think about your stormy morning,so I decided to ask

Oh, you miss understood,she told that cause i have found that we had met before already,we were classmates! And we were children then...so we hadn't recognized each other till this moment.

- Oh really? It make sense.

- Yes! And John, could I ask you one question too?

- You know,when I called you,your friend Tom picks up your phone and I thought that he lives with you...so I have thought that you are gay,as well.

- No I'm not! I like only women! Oh,Jenny,we probably miss understood each other,sorry about that.

- Oh its ok! Don't worry about that! i'm sorry too! But,John why you are interesting about this all?

John sits down at his desk.

- Well,i don't know how to explain it,i think,its because…

Lucie enters Jenny's hotel room and by this interrupts their conversation.

- Jenny,honey everyone is waiting for you already! Are you coming?

- Yes,give me one second,mom!


- I guess you have to go,lets talk later-says John.

- Yes, ok John

- Guests are sitting on the table and Jenny comes in her long red dress,Mark stands up and give her flowers.

- Jenny,you are gorgeous today as always Jenny takes flowers.

- Thank you Mark.

They hugs and sit on the table with other guests Everybody speaks,Mark's mom sits and speaks with Jenny's mother. Mark stands up from the table with jewelry box and at the same time Jenny gets message from John-I asked it because i like you.

- Jennifer, I want confess in love to you,you know you mean to me a lot and I know you from childhood,yes i had girlfriend but now i realise that i love you.

Beat. Lucie looks at Jenny and Jenny looks nervously at her.

- Will you marry me?- asks Mark.

Jenny stands up from the table with surprise.

- Mark,I really respect your choice to marry me!

- Yes sure.

- But i cant...Mark i really cant to marry you,to say to you yes, because...I'm not ready,i think i have feelings to someone else.

- But you not sure if that person likes you... the same as you like him or her!

- Him...

- Whatever, but we know each other from childhood and might be you not sure about your feelings but in the bottom of your heart might be...you have feelings to me,who knows.

- Mark,I'm sure that i cant marry you,but I'm sure that i love you...

Mark interrupts her, Lucie smiles.

- I love you too!

- As a friend

Beat. Lucie looks at Jenny.

- And yes, you right, I'm not sure about his feelings,but I know that at list he likes me too,and this is important for me.

- Jenny I see that you surprises by my suggestion...but really,you have to think about it.

Jenny looks at Mark.

- And for sure you could give me your answer later-joyfully says Mark.

Mark still stands up with the jewelry box and looks at everyone at Jenny's Birthday party and Jenny stands up affront of Mark.

- No Mark, I know for sure, I've already given you an answer.

Beat. Jenny gets out from the restaurant hall.

- I'm sorry-says Jenny by looking at all guests who is there. Mark looks at her with angry eyes Jenny runs away with a smile by music «Taylor Swift-Me» to the pool area at this hotel section and sits affront of the pool and takes her phone from her small bag and starts to text to John Jenny-John,I like you too!

Jenny sits in her office with a good mood and suddenly John knocks to her office while Jenny sits and typing something on her computer and suddenly she sees John and quickly stands up from her desk and John enters her office they hugs and while they hugs they are speaking.

*Veronika*

- Jenny I miss you.

- I miss you too...

Melissa suddenly sees how Jenny and John hugs ewhile she walks with another worker past Jenny's office.

- Is it Jenny hugs with John?

Mellisa and her colleague stand up affront of Jenny's office.

- I think yes-says with a smile another worker.

- Holy shit-says Mellisa with a surprise.

- Happy to see you.

- Me too Jennifer! I...received your message, so it is true?

- Yes John,its true,everything! Beat.

John takes out the jewelry box from his pocket,Jenny surprises and put her hands on her mouth.

- I guess you already realize what I want to ask you.

- O my God-exclaims Jenny.

John opens his jewelry box.

- Will you

Jenny interrups John.

- Yes!

A few weeks later, Jenny is in wedding dress by the mirror. Jenny's mother and Sammie stay behind her with glasses of wine.

- Oh dear its suits for you.

- Yes, take it!- confirms Sammantha.

Jenny nervously looks around her dress...

- Are you sure guys? I feel me fat in this... oh.

Jenny continues to look in the mirror.

- Do you think in another dress you will look differently?

Jenny and Sammie look at Lucie with a strange look.

- Oh thank you mom!

- What? I just guess that you like another dress too.

Shopping worker brings to them more Champagne.

- Would you like some more champagne?

- Oh thank you!

Beat. Shopping worker waits Sammie`s answer. Sammie looks at the Shopping worker.

- Yes!

Sammie takes a glass of champagne from a tray. Worker left.

- I start to like those wedding days...

- And Sammie drinks champagne. Jenny meanwhile she enters the dressing room and goes out in another more tight dress after a couple of seconds. Lucie and Sammie says-Wooow...

- Definitely this one!

Jenny smiles and turns around.

Jenny walks through the street with a dress in a bag.

- So,Sammie,dress we have bought.

- Now its time for wedding ring!-joyfully says Samantha.

- Yes...

They enters to jewelry shop.

Worker of jewerly shop welcomes them.

- Good Afternoon young ladies! You have wedding?

- Oh! I have,she is my classmate,who became a best friend to me,whom i met month ago!

- Wow,such a strange but interesting story!

- Yes... not a bride... but I wish I could be her...

Beat.

- Oh... Anyway! Come in!

Jenny and Sammie come closer to the showcase with rings. And Jenny shows on ring.

- Oh! This one! What do you think ha?

- He will like it...

- Could you take this ring for us please.

- Yes sure!

- Oh Sammie I'm so exited... finally i met my real love! And we will have a wedding day!

Sammie smiles to Jenny.

- Me too,because i could meet there my future girlfriend...

- Oh! By the way tommorow is my henparty.

Jenny slightly hit Sammi`s shoulder.

- You invited...

- Its gonna be hot there...i feel it!-smiles Samantha.

Jenny smiles to Samantha.

Jenny with her brother choose a cake for a wedding.

- What do you think,John gonna love chocolate or regular sponge cake?

- I don't know call and ask him, we live in modern world, its not difficult.

- I know Ben,but its so special day I want to make surprise for him... he doesn't call me to ask which dress better to buy...o my God... where is my bag with a dress!-wonders Jenny.

Jenny gives cake catalog to her brother and runs away with no comments.

- Yes Ben thank you that you will choose a cake for my wedding, I really appreciate it,what? Yes I love you too. Oh I will marry on my new worker,but not ex boyfriend, I'm so exited! I am so exited! i'm the best sister of all planet! i'm sexy lady...Oh yes-hysterical says to himself Ben.

Ben stands with a catalog in his hand portraying his sister, but he did not know that people in this store were sitting on the sofa behind him and when he turned back they looked at him intently and strangely that he was talking to himself.

- Oh…

Jenny comes with Mellisa and Sammie to the nightclub, wearing glasses at the same time by music-Britney Spears - Womanizer. Jenny has the rose ribbon „Bride to Be". They come to bar and sit down.

- I will have double wisky. What about you Sammie?

- I will have 5 shoots-says with surprise Sammie.

- You wanna be fully ready for our party?

- Right now yes.

Suddenly Sammie sees Christina

- Where is my shoots!-exclaims Samantha

- What happenes Sammie?

- Do you remember you told me about your ex worker Christina.

- Yes why you tell me about her on my bridenight?

- You know you have told me how she looks and that she always has red nails and red lipstick,so I think she is here-hysterical says Sammie.

- No way!- surprises Jenny.

Christina comes closer to Jenny.

- Oh oh oh, bride to be... isn't it a bit too early for you to get married...but I would like to say that it is too late for you.

- I don't care about your stupid opinion,because for you not late and not early to married. Marriage not for you.

- Jenny forget about her-says Sammie to Jenny.

- Yes you right!-answers Jennifer.

- Club its too good for you! You don't worth it!

- So you want to tell me that you could rock this club? Could you drink more than Me?

- Wow wow wow,Jenny,don't go down to her level. She don't worth it.

- Well,I won't

- You just afraid to lose Jenny.-says laughly Christina.

Jenny watches at her with angry eyes.

- You know what,I don't afraid! Let`s do it,cheater!

Jenny and Christina order ten and ten shoots of tequila and people around them watche on these two. Jenny starts first to drink three shoots all together. Christina drinks five shoots each 1 min. Jenny drinks five too and she has only two else,but Christina is already drunk and she has too drink 5 else.

- Come on honey you almost won! Jenny drunk 2 more without hands.

- No...says Christina.

Everybody claps to Jenny. Christina falls from chair.

- Somebody helps to stand up to this... cheater-says with a smile Jenny.

Jenny, Sammie and Mellisa walk all together and laugh.

- Oh you rock this club Jenny-says Sammie.

- Well, I just show her who is who.

They laughs all together and at that time Sammie pays attention to another bar.

- Hey guys,look at this, happy hour in the house! lets go there.

Everyone go there.

- I feel that this happy hour with good will not end-sighs Jenny.

Sammie on the bar desk shaking her head while Jenny and Mellisa on another side of bar for a drink Jenny turns around at the bar where everyone crowded around.

- Mellisa suddenly look at Sammie.

- Oh my God.

Jenny look at the same direction with Mellisa and sees there Sammie.

- Oh no,we need to take them out of there.

- Its too late Jenny-smiles Mellisa.

On the next day Jennifer wakes up at her bed with annoying alarm lying in pajamas with ducklings. And Sammie also there but Jenny does not remember it and doesn't see her yet. Shows a general view of how Jenny is sleeping and next to her on the floor is Sammie in pink glasses and in a T-shirt with a sign «Oh Yes». Jenny stands up from the bed and randomly sees Sammie.

- Sammie!

- What happens?-says sleepy Sammie

- Wake up!How you became in my apartement.

- I don't remember...yet

- We late at work wake up! John won't like that you sleep with me today.

- Only because I'm lesbian?

- Well yes dear,if you i won't be a lesbian he could react normally because we are just friends.

- But we are friends!-smiles Sammie.

- I know,but if he will know that you are here all night he could think differently, you know,only because you are lesbian!

- Oh might be,ok I'm leaving-sadly says Samantha.

- Yes its better because he gonna come soon,thank you dear.

- No problem!

Sammie goes out from Jenny's room. Jenny sits in her bed and tries to wake up and suddenly after a few minutes hears door bell.

- John its you? Jenny opens the door and there is Mark.

- Hello dear-flirty says Mark.

- Mark? Oh what are you doing here?-surprises Jenny.

- I'm here to speak with you.

- What about?

- About us,you know we should try again.

- No Mark I told you,you are the great person but the reason is not in yourself! Its in me! I love another person!

- I know,but we could just try,beause I love you,might be you could love me too, who knows! Or you already have someone?-hysterically says Mark.

- No,I mean not yet,I don't want to tell you,sorry.

Suddenly John calls to Jenny.

- Wait a minute Mark I have to answer.

- Hey dear,are you woke up-says John to Jenny by phone call.

- Hey John! Yes I'm at home.

- When I could come?-asks John.

- Whenever you want,might be in hour?-

- Not a good idea-says Mark

JOHN Who is there?

- Oh its my old friend

- Are you sure? You don't lie to me?

- No! John I'm sure!

- Can we continue our conversation please?

- Mark wait please! I told you!

John hangs up.

- Hello? John dear are you here? Oh no he hangs up the phone!

- Its him do you love? What he has that you love him and not me?

- Mark I cant explain you,you cant explain the reason when you love!I'm sorry. I'm not in the mood to talk with you, can you please leave?

Jenny closes her door.

- You make a mistake Jenny!I love you!-exclaims Mark.

Jenny sits in her living room crying and tries to call back to John but John doesn't answer

John sees message from Jenny and he is angry he doesn't reply.

enny stays affront of John's office she looks at him with sadness and he looks at her Jenny comes closer to him but he calls to someone and goes back to his office

Jenny comes to wait the elevator where also is John Jenny looks at John.

- You wont speak with your bride anymore?-hysterically says Jenny.

John looks at Jenny.

- My bride hasn't told me that she friends with some man who loves her.

- Listen,i don't care about him! Our moms are friends and its not my problem that he likes me!

Suddenly Mellisa calls Jenny from enny's company door and she turns to her and she did not have tI'me to go into the elevator with John.

- Jenny you forgot your wallet in your office!

- Oh thank you Mellisa! Give me one second Jenny turns back to the elevator and John already left,so Jenny sadly goes back to her company to take her wallet and when she turns back John already left and she sees how elevator closes.

Jenny walks down the stairs to her white car,then she opens her car. Jenny sits in her car b faster sit belt.

John sits in his car and left but Jenny doesn't see him.

Jenny drives up to the house where stands next to her house and smokes Sammie. Jenny gets out from her car and Sammie comes to her.

- Hey dude.-joyfully says Sammie.

- Hey Dudy.

- How are you?

- Oh...fine-sadly says Jenny.

- Are you sure?

- No! John is crazy he doesn't ant to listen me.

- Why? What happened?

This Mark comes from Miami for me! He always follows me everywhere!

- No way! O my God really? He is so romantic.

- Yesterday he was at my work,and there was John! He have seen Mark and he thought I lie to him

- Oh no...

- Oh yes!-hysterically says Jenny.

Beat.

- Look,might be we could check him,he knows you from the childhood,and he knows that you are rich girl .

- Yes,but he loves me from our childhood.

- Right,but as you know he had a relationships and on his facebook account he still has pictures with his ex girlfriend right?

- Right

- So might be he follows you to run your company because he is also a writer? Might be he want to be your husband only for that?

- Well...

- Because if he have been in love with you since his childhood and he is now 30 years old why he hadn't married you before?why he had girlfriend?

- Yes,might be you are right,I don't know.

- We should check it!

- Great idea! But how?

- Listen,you gonna call him and tell that you have some problems in your business and you want to lend money from him,and we will see what he gonna say then.

- I will do it!

Sammie smiles to Jenny.

Jenny stays in front of her window in her office and calls to Mark.

- Hey Mark!

Mark lies in the bed with his girlfriend.

- Oh hey Jenny,honey I glad to hear your voice.

- Oh Mark...where are you?Still in NYC?

- Yes,you know I'm here for you, and you can always rely on me.

- Yes,of course i know! Listen,I have something to tell you.

- Yes?-Mark surprises.

- I'm new in this business, and I have some financial problems there.

- Oh my love you know I could help you,and might be I could be, I mean...in your company,second hand you know,or even the second owner!

- What the...listen you will never be the owner of my grandmother's company,I just called you to lend you some money?And,you told me I could always rely on you, right?

- Yes,but I haven't told you that you could lend money from me.

- Oh really?no matter!don't call me anymore.

Jenny hangs up her phone with the smile.

Samantha sits in the class with her students.

- Richard as i told you,you are smart guy but math its not yours...you know,you should find where you are good at,I have heard that you good in music.

Richard looks at Sammie and suddenly Sammie notices that her phone rings, she takes her phone and sees that there is Jenny calls.

- Guys,read the first paragraph of the Pythagorean theorem and I will now return I have an important call.

One of the students tells to Sammie

- An important call from director?

- No,more important Beatrece.

Sammie stands up from her desk and gets out from the class.

Sammie calls back to Jenny.

- What's up?-joyfully asks Sammie.

- Hey! You are right! He follows me for my business!-tells Jenny.

Really?Oh i knew it.

Jenny is reading her new magazine and speaks on phone with Sammie.

- And you know what? He asks me if he could be second owner of my magazine! its crazy! I'm so surprise...and he asks me this before my question you know.

- See I told you! Oh my God.

- hope John will forgive me,because its not my idea that Mark has come to New York...

- Yes,i hope too honey. Beat.

Sammie looks at the class window where her students turns on the music in class and dancing,while Sammie not there.

- Oh I'm sorry i have to go back to class

- Ok dear! Have a nice day! Thank you for the help!-says with a smile Jenny.

- You too.

Jenny hangs up the phone,and she dials John's phone number but suddenly decides to close her phone and continuous with her work...she drinks coffee. Then Jenny turns on her computer and sees there message from John - Dear Jennifer, i,Jonathan Peronetti want to tell you that i really appreciate your opportunity to me to work with you but i don't feel me comfortable to work with you,its not problem in yourself, its problem in me. So officially want to ask you to be fired. Best Regards,John Jenny reads it with tears in her eyes and she calls to John to ask what happened and he doesn't answer.

John sits with his friend Tom in his kitchen on the table with the breakfast and cups of tea.

- John,did you quit Jenny's company?

- I made right decision.

- You even don't know who is this Mark for real!

John drinks a cup of tea.

- I already made a first step.

- Good!

- I engaged her.

- Oh really?

- Yes but I need to find out more information about this Markyou are right, but now I can not work in her company.

Tom drink a cup of tea .

- You want to see me suffer?

- Of course not!

- So,that's why i dont wont to work there,I will find a new work.

- But you will not speak with her anymore?-exclaims Tom

- Well if i wont find that Mark is her love or boyfriend, whatever I will speak with her,if not,I will told her that she is not my bride anymore.

- think that if Jenny engaged with you it means that she doesn't has anything with Mark you know,she loves you.

- Ihope so-sighs John.

- John,what if we could go somewhere today not to think about it all to forgot bad moments?

- Ok lets go,good idea.

- Might be mwe could go to that coffee where I'm usually go with my girlfriend?

- Baby Cafe?

- Yes!

- But why you guys don't go now?

Oh,she told me that she always doesn't has any tI'me,she works a lot.

- Ok lets go

- Yes

John and Tom stand up from the table.

John and Tom walking on the street to the cafe way.

- I like such New York's daytI'me,a lot of yellow cars,fashion people, a lot of restaraunts,you know.

John looks around .

- Yes...it was always my dream to come here,and I guess dreams comes true,might be not all of them but some of them for sure,and I'm here ! in a big apple!

- Why not all of them?The women whom you love, has feelings to you too.

- Tom,please don't remind me about her,I'm not sure about her feelings to me.

- Jennifer Jennifer Jennifer!

- Tom!

- Oh look,its that caffee! Lets go!

Tom and John go to this cafe and suddenly Tom sees his girlfriend sitting with Mark! and Tom stops abruptly ahead of John.

- What happens Tom?

Tom still looks at caffee's window.

- She is there.

- Who?

- My girlfriend.

- Oh nice!-joyfully says John.

Lets go, you will introduce me to her.

- No,she sits with Mark.

- Oh my God,with that Mark?

- Yes.

- Oh,I'm so sorry.

John hugs Tom.

- Its ok,at least i know who is she and you know who is Jenny.

- Yes,now I see that this Mark cheats on Jenny but Jenny doesn't cheat on me

- Ok lets go,I wont never go to this cafe ever.

- Lets find another cafe.

- What about bar?

- Much better,do you want a beer?

- Sure! Double.

Describes how they walk on the New York's street.

Jenny goes from her work to her car and there John waits her with the flowers Jenny Jenny stops at a distance from her car and looks at John John next to her car looks at her. Jenny slowly coming to John. Jenny stands in front of John.

- I'm so sorry. Beat. Please forgive me! Jenny! I was so angry that Mark always follows you.

Jenny looks at him. She takes his hands,and John looks at her hands and also takes her hands

- I will-says Jenny.

John smiles.

Only because you said sorry-smiles Jenny.

- Thank you,boss.

John gives to her flowers,she takes them.

- You know Jenny, I have seen Mark with Tom's girlfriend.

- Oh really?-laughly says Jenny.

- Yes,my love,its not funny.

- I know,but the fact that Mark wants to marry me for my business its so funny.

- This yes.

- Oh John,you don't know how much I happy that you realize that I'm not lying to you.

John kisses her hand and looks at her.

- Jennifer,could i ask it again?

- What?

- Will you marry me?

- Yes!

It shows how they sit in Jenny's car together by music-Ariana Grande -Imagine.

A few weeks later

It shows New York city, birds are singings, white limousine,and it shows closer view how Jenny gets out from this car in her long white wedding dress,it shows general view how security gives her a hand so she can gets out of her limousine. Jennifer smiles to him and also her waits already Mellisa and Sammie to enter together to the wedding hall. They go together.

- Jennifer your marriage ceremony will be in an hour you still have tIime to get ready.

Jennifer climbs up the stairs in front of the girls and after Melissa's speech,she turns around and looks at her with a smile.

- Thank you dear.

Sammie looks at Mellisa.

- Mellisa,you are not at work,today I'm the bridesmaid-says Sammie.

Jennifer laughs.

- Today everyone could give me advice girls-says Jennifer.

They enters the wedding hall where reception ask them.

- Hello! My name is Jennifer Walter! i have a wedding here in Raddison!

- Good Morning Jennifer! Congratulations, your wedding on the third floor.

- Thank you.

- Yes thank you!-says Sammie.

They look around and go up by the elevaator.

Jenny sits and make up artist makes for her make up then comes to her room her mom.

Knock knock. Jenny opens her eyes and smiles.

- Mom!

- Oh Jenny I can not believe my girl is a bride today!

- Yes,finally!

They laughs and hugs.

- How is your mood today?

Make up artist looks at Lucie with a smile.

- As I see,while I make make up for her,she is so happy,I haven't seen such a happy bride.

Lucie looks at Jenny.

- Yes,she is so happy,I haven't see her so happy such a long period.

Make up artist done with her work,she looks at Jenny.

- Ok we done,princess!

- Thank you very much.

- Welcome.

Jenny turns to the mirror. Lucie straightens her dressю Jenny and her mom looks at the mirror together.

- I told you that your happiness will search you,you just have to wait.

- I guess you right mom-joyfully says Jennifer.

- And here we are, in front of the mirror in the wedding room.

Sammie and Melisa walk around the hotel.

- Oh need to use restroom-says Melissa.

- Ok I will be here.

Mellisa goes to the restroom .

Suddenly Sammie sees her ex girlfriend. Alicia walks near her with John,but they don't see Sammie because Sammie hides.

- My lovely brother i can not believe that you marry today.

- Yes me too! But I'm so happy.

- I know!

Sammie surprises and runs to Jenny's room.

Jenny take a pictures of herself when suddenly comes Sammie. She stands in front of the Jenny with surprise at her face. Jenny looks at her.

- What happened?

- My…

- Who?

- My ex girlfriend is the sister of John! Beat. Jenny sits down with surprise in her eyes.

Can you imagine this?-says laughly Sammie.

- Are you sure?

- Yes! I have seen them right now,she told to John-Oh my little brother...I'm so happy,my little brother marries today. Jenny smiles and stands up.

- This is amazing Sammie! You know what it means?

- What? JENNY That she is your destiny! Beat.

- I hope so.

- This is a labyrinth of love!

They smile to each other Suddenly Melissa comes to their room.

- Everybody is waiting for you Jenny-says Melissa.

- Ok one second please.

Jenny looks at Sammie.

- Ok Sam! its your chance.

- What do you mean?

- Listen,you should come to her and tell how much you miss her.

- Wow-smiles Melissa.

- Ok i will try.

Jenny smiles.

- Might be its a real sign.

- Yes

- Ok Ladies lets go.

They left wedding room.

- Girls, I'm so exited.

- Me too-says laughly Sammie.

- By the way if you are interesting i like Tom,I think he is handsome.

- Wow Mellisa

Jenny and Sammie are laughing.

- What? I also want to love.

- You will.

Mellisa smiles to her.

- Ok young lady you wait here and we will be inside.

- Ok,oh by the way my dad gonna be today here.

- Oh my God really? I thought you didn't communicate with your father.

- Yes i didn't,but he has found me in facebook and told me that he is sorry that he hasn't spoken with me before,and I…

- You forgive him?-exclaims Sammie.

- All my 25 years I wanted to find him but my mom hasn't told me about him,but I decided to invite him on my wedding.

- No way!-says Sammie.

- Yes! He gonna come so soon!

- But your mum knows about it?

- No,but its my dad and I'm adult person, I have the right to communicate with him!

Suddenly Jenny's dad comes to her behind her. Melissa and Sammie go inside the wedding hall.

- Yes, you have rights to see me dear daughter.-says George.

Jenny turns back and sees her dad.

- Oh, thanks for coming,dad.

They hugs. her dad He takes her hand.

- Lets go,to your new life Jenny?

- Yes-Jenny smiles.

Doors are opens by music Beethoven and Jenny enters with her dad,everyone stand up and John waits her at the altar Jenny walks and smiles to Sammie,while Sammie looks at her suddenly her look meets by chance with her ex-girlfriend Alicia And Lucie surprises by seeing her ex- husband

- Ben,why your dad is here? Ben-brother of Jenny looks at his dad.

- Oh my God, really don't know mom. George gives Jenny to John,and sits down. Jenny and John takes each other's hands.

- Do you agree, Jennifer Walter to take John Perruni as a husband?-says registrar of registry.

- Yes!

- Do you agree,John Perunni to take Jennifer Walter in wife?

- Yes! And again yes and yes!-joyfully says John.

John wears a ring from Tom's hands on Jenny and Jennifer wears a ring on him from Sammie's hands.

- According to the laws of the United States of America, i declare you a husband and wife! Jenny and John kisses,everyone clups,plays wedding music. Sammie clups and at the same time Alicia goes to Sammie.

- Hello!

Sammie surprisely turns to her

- Hey!

- I haven't know that we would meet up again-flirty says Alisa to Sammie.

- And I cant believe that you are John's sister.

- Yes I'm.

Jenny and John look at them with a smile.

- I miss you Alicia.

Alicia touches Sammie's hair.

- I miss you too.

- Can I ask a question?

- Yes.

Do you have a girlfriend?

- No.

Beat.

- And...what about you?

- No-smiles Sammie.

They kisses by music–«Justin Bieber- sorry».

John and Jenny are dancing in the middle of the hall and Mellisa sits at the wedding table and looks how Jenny and John dance with a smile when suddenly Tom comes to her.

- Hello,you are so beautifull.

Mellisa looks at him.

- Oh thank you!

- My name is Tom,nice to meet you.

Tom held out his hand to Mellisa.

- Melissa,nice to meet you too! Melissa held out her hand to him too.

- Mellisa,such a beautiful name.

- Thank you-smiles Melissa.

- Could i invite you to dance?

- Yes.

Melissa stands up and they start to dance.

Jenny's dad suddenly comes to Lucie.

- Hello Lucie.

Lucie looks at him.

- You found your daughter

- Of course! it is not her fault that we were divorced and then I changed you, yes, but this was not a reason to divorce. Beat.

You know,you have son also! Look its him,i called him Ben.

Really? Lucie meet Ben to him .

- I'm so happy person-joyfully says George.

He goes to his son and they talk and hug each ohter. Lucie smiles. John and Jenny smiles to each other during the dance.

- I love you

- I love you more! You know if i wouldn't come to New York I hadn't met you.

- And if I wont go to your work I wouldn't meet you too,Jenny.

She smiles.

- Yes,its true.

- You know I become in love with you from the first sight.

- Actually,me too!- admits John.

Jenny smiles.

Shows general view of the wedding hall and then general view of New York And words of autor Love,like the butterfly,if you wont catch her once you will catch her later. Jenny and John believe in the destiny cause their destiny is the labyrinth of love, from which they both went together, holding hand in hand and never parting.

Printed in the United States
By Bookmasters